Put Be~~ginning~~ Readers on the Right Track with

The All Aboard Reading ~~...~~ ning readers. Written
by noted authors and illustr~~ated...~~ hat children really
want to read—books to excite their imagination, expand their interests, make them
laugh, and support their feelings. With fiction and nonfiction stories that are high
interest and curriculum-related, All A~~...~~ y
young reader. And with four differen
lets you choose which books are most
growing abilities.

Picture Readers

Picture Readers have super-simple te~~xt...~~ appearing as rebus
pictures. At the end of each book are 24 flash cards—on one side is a rebus picture;
on the other side is the written-out word.

Station Stop 1

Station Stop 1 books are best for children who have just begun to read. Simple
words and big type make these early reading experiences more comfortable. Picture
clues help children to figure out the words on the page. Lots of repetition throughout
the text helps children to predict the next word or phrase—an essential step in
developing word recognition.

Station Stop 2

Station Stop 2 books are written specifically for children who are reading with help.
Short sentences make it easier for early readers to understand what they are reading.
Simple plots and simple dialogue help children with reading comprehension.

Station Stop 3

Station Stop 3 books are perfect for children who are reading alone. With longer
text and harder words, these books appeal to children who have mastered basic
reading skills. More complex stories captivate children who are ready for more
challenging books.

In addition to All Aboard Reading books, look for All Aboard Math Readers™
(fiction stories that teach math concepts children are learning in school); All Aboard
Science Readers™ (nonfiction books that explore the most fascinating science topics in
age-appropriate language); and All Aboard Poetry Readers™ (funny, rhyming poems
for readers of all levels).

All Aboard for happy reading!

GROSSET & DUNLAP
Published by the Penguin Group
Penguin Group (USA) Inc., 375 Hudson Street, New York, New York 10014, USA
Penguin Group (Canada), 90 Eglinton Avenue East, Suite 700,
Toronto, Ontario M4P 2Y3, Canada
(a division of Pearson Penguin Canada Inc.)
Penguin Books Ltd., 80 Strand, London WC2R 0RL, England
Penguin Group Ireland, 25 St. Stephen's Green, Dublin 2, Ireland
(a division of Penguin Books Ltd.)
Penguin Group (Australia), 250 Camberwell Road, Camberwell, Victoria 3124, Australia
(a division of Pearson Australia Group Pty. Ltd.)
Penguin Books India Pvt. Ltd., 11 Community Centre, Panchsheel Park,
New Delhi—110 017, India
Penguin Group (NZ), 67 Apollo Drive, Rosedale, North Shore 0632, New Zealand
(a division of Pearson New Zealand Ltd.)
Penguin Books (South Africa) (Pty.) Ltd., 24 Sturdee Avenue,
Rosebank, Johannesburg 2196, South Africa

Penguin Books Ltd., Registered Offices:
80 Strand, London WC2R 0RL, England

ISBN 978-0-448-45167-1   10 9 8 7 6 5

All Aboard Reading™

with 24 Flash Cards!

PICTURE READER

SkippyjonJones

THE GREAT BEAN CAPER

Based on the *Skippyjon Jones* series created by

J U D Y   S C H A C H N E R

 bounced up and

down on his big-boy  .

As he bounced he said,

"Oh, I'm Skippyjon Jones,

and I bounce with the best.

No one dares cross me,

I'll beat any pest."

Then  began to

dig through his  .

Out came a and a

 . Finally, he found

what he was looking for . . .

Skippyjon put on his  and tied on

his 👓 . Then he

walked toward his 🚪 .

Inside, a  hissed. A  squeaked. And Los

Chimichangos waited for

Skippyjon. "Ay, Skippito,"

said Don Diego, a purple

. "It is good you are

here. El Bumblebeeto has

stolen our !"

"Holy guacamole!"

Skippito Friskito cried.

"We must get them back!"
 grabbed his

and an . And off the

muchachos went in his

.

" 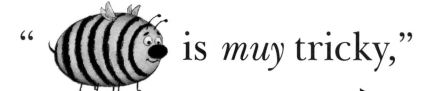 is *muy* tricky,"

Don Diego said. But  wasn't worried.

"There are **8** of us, and

just **1** of him," Skippito

Friskito said as the

sailed down the  .

"Keep a lookout, *perritos!*"

At last the *muchachos*

reached an  . A

trail of  led away

from the water. *"Vamanos!"*

cried Skippito.

Skippito and his *amigos* found  resting in a  . "Ay, Bumblebeeto," Skippito called out, "give Los Chimichangos back their  !" But El Bumblebeeto didn't hear him. He was asleep!

Skippito quietly climbed

up the . Then he

began to pile the

into his . Suddenly,

El Bumblebeeto opened

his .

 grabbed the

and raced down the

 . Los Chimichangos

chanted, "Skippito is a

hero!" But just kept

running. He was in such a

hurry to get away that he

crashed right into . . .

Mama Junebug Jones.

"Come on, Mr. Fuzzy Pants,"  said. "Let's go get some

dinner. I made  !"

bed/*cama*

Skippyjon
Jones

ball/*pelota*

toy chest/
caja de juguete

cape/*capa*

car/*coche*

closet/*armario*	mask/ *máscara*
mouse/*ratón*	snake/ *serpiente*
beans/*frijoles*	dog/*perro*

oar/*remo*

sword/*espada*

El Bumblebeeto

boat/*barco*

one/*uno*

eight/*ocho*

island/*isla*

river/*río*

bag/*bolso*

tree/*árbol*

Mama
Junebug
Jones

eye/*ojo*